The Best Day Ever

Originated by Polly Dunbar

WALKER BOOKS
AND SUBSIDIARIES
LONDON · BOSTON · SYDNEY · AUCKLAND

GREENWICH LIBRARIES

3 8028 02101215 5

It was morning in the Yellow House,
the start of a great day.

Tilly and her friends were painting pictures.

Soon it was time to play dressing-up.

"I'm a fireman," said Tumpty.

"And I'll be an astronaut!" said Tilly.

Tilly brought sandwiches and everyone
sat down to a delicious feast.

"I'm hungry," said Doodle.
"Bitey, bitey!"

Then everyone went outside to play tiddly-winks.

The buttons were too
small for Tumpty, so Tilly
found something better.

Everyone had a grand time.

At dance time, Tiptoe did the petal dance.

"I don't want this day to end!" said Hector.

"The best thing we can do," said Tilly,
"is remember everything about today.

And I have an idea!"

The friends decided to make a scrapbook.
Everyone wanted to include their
favourite part of the day.

Tumpty liked
tiddly-winks.

Pru's favourite thing
was dressing-up.

Doodle liked lunch, and
Hector loved dancing and painting.

Tiptoe's favourite
was the petal dance.

"The thing I liked best was being together with all my friends," said Tilly.

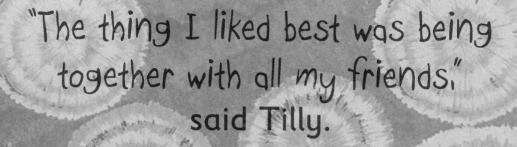

"Come on!
Let's be scraps in the scrapbook!"

Tilly painted her hand and stamped it in the book. Everyone else did, too. It was the perfect way for everyone to be together in the scrapbook.

"I think tomorrow's going to be
the best day ever, too," Tumpty said.
"And the day after that!" said Doodle.

First published 2013 by Walker Books Ltd, 87 Vauxhall Walk, London SE11 5HJ

2 4 6 8 10 9 7 5 3 1

© 2012 JAM Media and Walker Productions
Based on the animated series TILLY AND FRIENDS, developed and produced by Walker Productions and JAM Media
from the Walker Books 'Tilly and Friends' by Polly Dunbar. Licensed by Walker Productions Ltd.

This book has been typeset in Gill Sans and Boopee.

Printed in China

All rights reserved. No part of this book may be reproduced, transmitted or stored in an information retrieval system
in any form or by any means, graphic, electronic or mechanical, including photocopying, taping and recording,
without prior written permission from the publisher.

British Library Cataloguing in Publication Data:
a catalogue record for this book is available from the British Library

ISBN 978-1-4063-4530-8

www.walker.co.uk

See you again soon!